The Blossoms of Summer

Also by Cecilia Tan

Bent for Leather
Black Feathers
Daron's Guitar Chronicles, Vol. 1-13
Edge Plays
The Hot Streak
Mind Games
The Prince's Boy
Royal Treatment
Silk Threads
Telepaths Don't Need Safewords
The Velderet
Watch Point
White Flames

The Magic University Series
The Siren and the Sword
The Tower and the Tears
The Incubus and the Angel
The Poet and the Prophecy
Spellbinding: Tales from the Magic University
Christmas Magic

The Struck by Lightning Series
Slow Surrender
Slow Seduction
Slow Satisfaction

The Secrets of a Rock Star series
Taking the Lead
Wild Licks
Hard Rhythm

The Blossoms of Summer

A Tale of the Forbidden Flowers

Cecilia Tan

The Blossoms of Summer
Copyright © 2023, 2024 by Cecilia Tan
All Rights Reserved

ISBN 978-1-963897-16-6

Originally published in 2023 as part of the *Hot & Sticky* compilation from Passionate Ink. Passionate Ink is an organization dedicated to erotica and erotic romance writers.

Cover design: The Author Buddy

blog.ceciliatan.com

Published by Cecilia Tan
39 Hurlbut St
Cambridge MA 02138

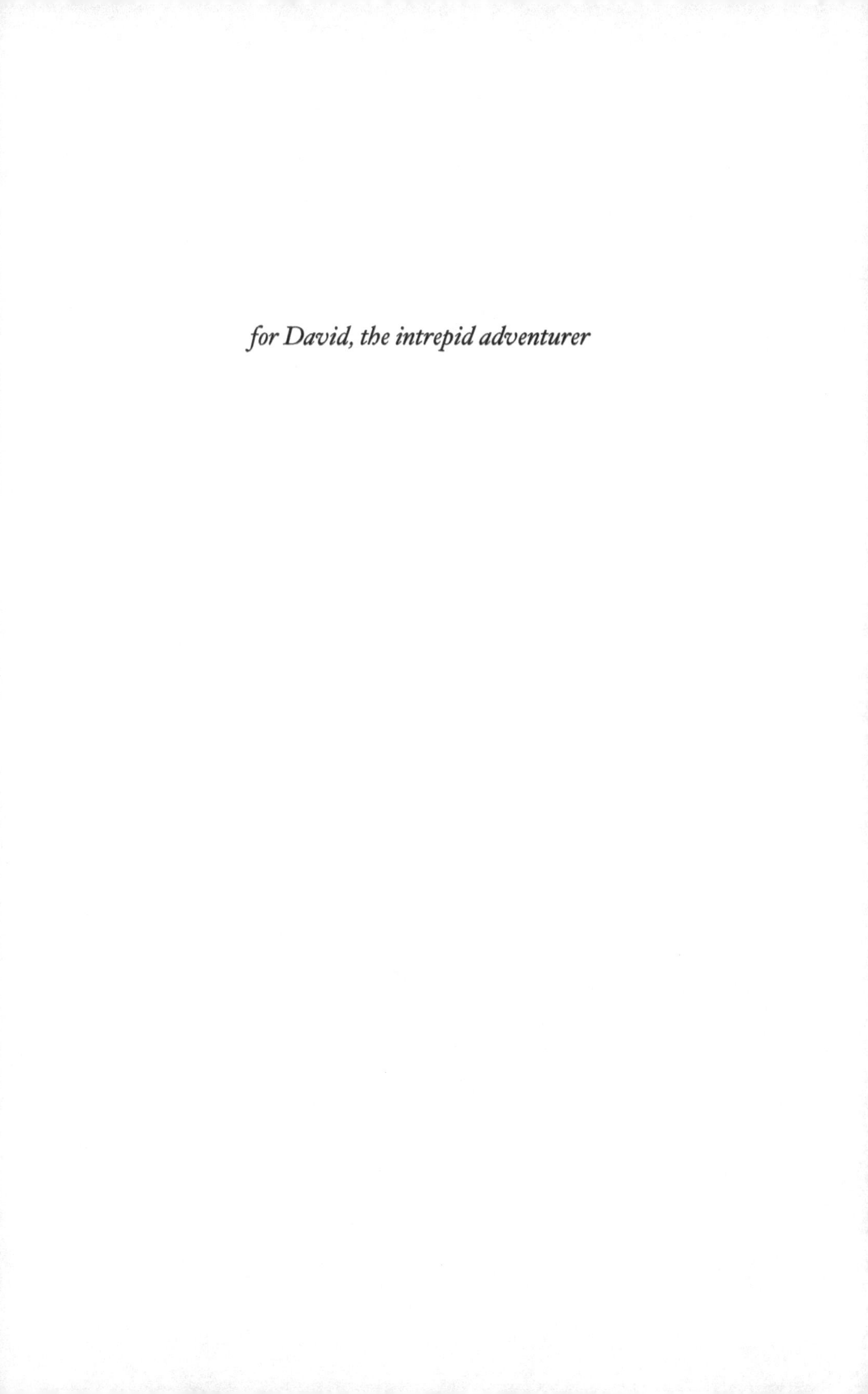

for David, the intrepid adventurer

Dearest Livia,

I write you today with some of the most momentous news imaginable, and yet my heart is heavy, the reason for which you shall soon discover. Never think for a moment that you have left my thoughts. Indeed, our future together is foremost in my mind when considering the proposal I have on my writing table, delivered to me not an hour ago by a most esteemed personage representing the Continental Occident Company.

Livia, my darling, you know the only reason I have hesitated to broach the subject of our engagement with your father has been my uncertainty about the standing in society with which I shall represent you and our future family. I should never wish to doom us to an eternal winter, forever peering into the windows at the firelight warmth and merriment of those in society whilst we shiver, forever outside of that realm! That fear, however, shall be banished forever should I succeed at the task being set forth before me. Indeed, I believe fortune has delivered me this chance, that I might woo you and wed you as a gentleman.

And so we come to it. The Company wishes for me to undertake an expedition to the Far East to retrieve rare exotics. The rose, the forsythia, the azalea, and other ornamentals have taken root in our gardens as common as common can be, but did you know, my own most beautiful blossom, that every one of those beauties came from Canton's once impassable mountains? And there, more treasures await! The Company shall employ me to retrieve the so-called "Blossoms of Summer" by airship. Can you imagine? More rare than the rose, more delicate than the forsythia, more colorful than the azalea, and therefore "forbidden" to be removed from their native lands—until now. These specimens must be truly incredible, and merely to lay eyes on one would be a blessing the likes of which a scientist can only dream. Except that I am the fortunate soul who has been chosen to lovingly uproot these flowers and transport them—alive!—back to the Company's herbariums.

Like the hardy horticultural adventurers before me, I shall be rewarded: the stewardship of the Botanical Society's property in Somerset awaits me upon my successful return. There, I shall have the run of both the extensive gardens and the eternal summer of the greenhouses. The position also includes a charming manor, a generous stipend, and entré into the most exclusive circles.

It shall be everything you dreamed of, my darling, and more.

I expect the journey to take the better part of a year, perhaps two. The details of the expedition will not be divulged until I commit myself to the mission, but my forbears have all achieved their dreams, including some whom I humbly submit are not half the botanists that I am! Such a protracted absence from you is the sole factor which troubles me about this expedition, and yet as my airship sails over the tea terraces I shall sleep well, knowing that our reunion shall be as sweet as a late August persimmon.

Yours eternally,

Robert

Mr. John Edwards, Esq.
No. 7 Thackeray Row

I once again find myself in need of your sage advice, dear Jack. If the snow does not deter you, please meet me at the Parham House club tonight after supper? I have something to speak of I dare not put into a letter, and my excitement over the opportunity I have been given may be clouding my judgment. I need your cool head and knowledge of society once again, but perhaps soon I may at last repay you for all the kindnesses you have visited upon a poor specimen such as myself. The Company is seeking to employ me, yet every answer they give raises more questions. More than that I cannot say until we speak. I await your reply.

Respectfully,
Robert Meriweather
Horticultural Fellow, Second Class

Dear Diary,

Assuming the ice storm which has gripped the city has abated by tomorrow, shortly shall I set sail on a voyage the like of which I have previously only ever dreamt. In preparation I have re-read the works of the great adventuring naturalists, in hopes that my own name might soon stand among theirs in the canon of botanical literature. The Company is sending me on a most specific errand. But—perhaps in exchange for the danger in which I may place my person— they have granted me the rights to whatever additional discoveries I might make along the way. Who knows what incredible birds or insects or medicinal herbs I might chance across? I am determined to keep as thorough notes as I can. Perhaps I will find a subject worthy of presentation at the Royal Horticultural Society, or even the International Naturalists Symposium. Oh what prestige could be mine should Fate present me with such!

My only reservations remain in the couched terms with which my instructions have been presented, which are sufficiently vague to cause concern that misinterpretation on my part might result in failure to fulfill them. All attempts at greater clarity were brushed aside by my superiors with such deliberateness that I must conclude they expect I may have to conduct myself in a less than gentlemanly manner!

And yet, what unspeakable acts could they possibly expect a botanist to perform? Is it possible that when they direct me to "retrieve" a specimen, they in fact intend for me to abscond like a thief in the night? Preposterous,. When it comes to *botanical* riches, unlike a treasure looted from a king's tomb, a cutting from a flower, lovingly nurtured, harms not the mother plant and yet increases the bounty for all.

I must set aside my reservations. I must. For I am committed to this course.

The Most Honorable and Esteemed Terence Featherstone
Continental Occident Company
Wickham House
Grace Park

Dear Sir,

I thank you again for this most wondrous and generous opportunity to advance the science of botany and the acclaim of crown and Company. I trust that you have been receiving my regular reports of our voyage as we have crossed the paths of several Company couriers, but in case of mishap, I shall recap quickly my travels to this point. The oversea portion of the voyage proceeded marvelously except for the one extraordinary storm we encountered during the spring thaw, and both icebergs and sudden squalls had to be dodged, and I give full commendation to the captain and crew of HMS Zenobia in delivering both my person and the airship safely to landfall.

The airship Queen of the Horizon is now fully assembled and ready for our inland journey, and I am pleased to report that we have managed to secure a territorial map that should aid us in navigating clear of the rebel-held areas. Along with the map we have secured a translator of some repute who can both read and write our language, and who can guide our communications with the remote chieftains as necessary. Our intention is to set sail clandestinely from our moorings tomorrow night under moonless skies. I expect we shall be able to arrive in good time for summer flowers to be in full bloom.

Incredibly, some of our own colleagues in port have disparaged the existence of the Tsang Valley as a myth! I can only assume that men of such good standing approach with skepticism anything they have not seen with their own eyes, and given the impassable nature of the mountains, the obscurity of the tongue which is spoken in the countryside, and the dangers of the travail on foot or even on river—from both pirates and governmental agents attempting to bar the way of any foreigner into forbidden territory—they have understandably steered clear. This is all to the good of the Company, for if the reports of your agents are true, the specimens you have sent me to retrieve shall indeed be prized beyond all imagining, or at least beyond the imagining of such petty-minded men whose dreams do not venture much beyond their next meal nor the walls of their own gardens.

I wish to reiterate at this time, honorable Sir, that I shall do my utmost to carry out the instructions I have been given. Though these instructions at times leave themselves open to multiple interpretations and certain ambiguities, I trust that I have grasped the subtleties of the task at hand, and that so long as I present a reasonable case for having adhered to the instructions, that all shall be well and that the Directors shall be pleased with my work.

I look forward to the day I return from the land of perpetual summer when I may present you with your very own "forbidden" blossom,

your servant,

Rbt. Meriweather

Mr. John Edwards, Esq.
No. 7 Thackeray Row

Dear Jack,

I know there is no hope of you receiving this letter much before my own return from my travels, so I write you to console myself and try to hear your wise voice in my head, dear friend. And should anything befall me, you, at least, will have some slim chance of knowing what truly occurred. The Queen of the Horizon is a true marvel of teak and canvas and steam and I write you tonight from so far above the Earth that my very spirit might soar to Heaven. Perhaps it is this fancy which has my concerns astir.

You are the only man aside from me and those privileged inside the Company to have seen my orders. I am to be responsible for the "inspection, collection, and transport of five 'blossoms of summer' a.k.a. the 'Forbidden Flowers'" including the "maintenance of the specimens' health and discovery of their unique needs, such that the specimens shall be delivered in the prime of beauty," and this is the part that now concerns me: "for the benefit of private investors under utmost discretion." Have you heard through society talk, I wonder, whom these investors might be? I fear, reading over the tone of the instructions and what I perceive to be the future of the specimens I collect, that unlike the beauties brought by Mr. Fortune and his predecessors which were cultivated and celebrated in gardens across the land, that these may be kept secret, accessible only to an anointed few. Indeed, I am taken to understand that there may be something of a diplomatic incident were the word to get out, and following so quickly on the heels of the Opium War as we are, no one wants that. So the need for secrecy has been well-impressed upon me. And yet, I worry.

Of course if they are honorable men, the Company's directors will appoint me as promised to the position I covet, and all shall be well in my world, but I cannot help but worry that disappointment will follow when my discoveries are not trumpeted like those of the botanist adventurers before me. And beyond that, of course, I worry most that if true secrecy is to be maintained, that my own silence can ultimately be bought only with the ultimate price.

Oh, but these are the flights of fancy of a man unmoored from the Earth! No one shall murder me over flowers! Wish me luck, Jack, for tomorrow I set foot on soil only rarely trod by any Occidental foot!

Yrs,

Rbt.

To the Honorable, Esteemed, Heavenly, et cetera et cetera Chieftain of the Tsang Mountain Pass—

It is with humblest gratitude that I send my servant and translator, who goes by the name of Wu, in respect for your tradition that none bearing Occidental blood should pass through your gates, to negotiate for the transfer of five of your finest specimens to my airship, which is moored in the tea fields at the foothills.

Dear Diary,

We have arrived in the most breathtakingly beautiful land, though it is strange to the eye! We are accustomed to mountainsides covered with forest but crowned at the peak with bare rock. Some of the terrain here is of that style, but there is also the opposite: red sandstone abuttments rise steeply up, entirely stone, yet crowned on top by greenery! I have never before seen the like.

I had taken the term "the land of perpetual summer" to be hyperbole, but no, it is quite literal. But for a few species that flower only in the spring—such as the ornamental cherry—the fruit falls ripe from the trees here all year round. The foothills are terraced by tea plantings which yield three harvests a year, each season imbuing a different character and flavor. While scientifically speaking I knew such variation should be possible, it is the first time I have beheld this distinction with all my senses, taste included.

I have yet to lay eyes on the "blossoms of summer" and I have been told that it may be some time before we receive a reply to our entreaty. The heat, which I expected to find oppressive, is tempered by the mountainous breezes, making each day a delight, but also contributing to a certain languidness of the people. Perhaps when ones days are always long, the habit of hurrying never takes hold?

In this land, one cannot strut about in quite so much clothing as we are accustomed without being overcome by the temperature, and some of the airmen have adopted the local custom of wearing a long tunic, open at the neck, that allows for full circulation of a cooling breeze. The captain has stated that he allows it so long as they do not expose themselves indecently.

I for my part have retained my trousers, but the only cloth that sits around my neck now is one dampened and sweetened with the local perfume, such that it tickles the senses with invigorating and cooling zephyrs. The airmen heartily extol my new manner of dress, remarking that my lack of shirt proves the long months of travail have transformed me from pale, bookish weakling into a bronzed Prussian. They could not know, of course, that one reason I was seduced by Botany rather than one of the other Sciences was that I indeed preferred the invigorating effects of outdoor toil over the enervating effects of laboratories or libraries where my colleagues in Chemistry and Mathematics are required to pass their time. Never let it be said that I was loath to get my hands dirty! I accept the crew's chiding in the spirit in which it is meant: they now accept me as one of them.

We passed the afternoon today in a shade pavilion constructed of bamboo and silk by the locals alongside our mooring, sipping herbaceous concoctions cooled in the streams which run from the mountaintops, utterly at our leisure. I am anxious that our mission should advance as quickly as possible, but until our messenger returns, there is naught to do but wait and enjoy the hospitality that is offered.

The Most Honorable and Esteemed Terence Featherstone
Continental Occident Company
Wickham House
Grace Park

Dear Sir,

I write you today in the full knowledge that my letter may likely not reach you before my task is complete, but in the hopes of reporting and recording impressions that maybe helpful to future trade with this baffling region of the world.

We arrived at the pass to the Tsang Valley some days ago, and for one thing, I have found that monks run the place. The restrictions against our entry to certain areas are not, in fact, a matter of simple law or decree as they are in the areas where the Mandarins rule, but of spiritual purity. Negotiation with them has been somewhat difficult in that they have little to profit by from our goods or money, and so I have had to be exceedingly creative in my promises to them.

The good news is that they are not in the least hostile, and have openly banqueted and celebrated with myself and the crew of the Horizon—outside their monastic gates, of course. I have still not laid eyes on a single specimen of "forbidden flower" but Wu, the translator, assures me that deep inside the massive lamasery there are sights of such stunning beauty they will make a man fall to his knees.

Another thing I shall note for the edification of future expeditions; do not be fooled by the seeming bucolic simplicity of these folk. Though many mendicants and clergy of our own land have lacked literacy and education, these monks are more in the vein of the great Linnaeus. I have been startled repeatedly here by the intimate knowledge of mathematics and engineering that all present seem to possess, from the most holy of their wise men down to the lowliest initiate tilling rice on the hillside. It was this observation that led to the single negotiation that was ultimately successful, one which I hope you will approve of heartily, as they refused nearly all goods we offered. In truth, they stated they live in paradise, and what need have they of gold or goods such as we could provide?

Not a shilling of the Company's currency will they take. Indeed, the only item they truly crave is knowledge, and once this fact was fully grasped by me, I was able to rescue the negotiation by offering the one area of expertise they lack. Hence, we are allowing them to map out every inch of the Horizon. The monks are quite peaceful, but they fear the rebellion that is spreading from the coast, and they quite quickly grasp that air power could easily be used in their defense.

The only sticking point in the negotiation that remains is my insistence that we must leave as soon as they have delivered the five specimens to me, in order to maintain their freshness. They have assured me that various herbs and so on must be kept thriving alongside them for their health, which is a fascinating discovery in itself! Apparently the proximity of certain plants will keep the blossoms of summer free of disease? The translation is too imprecise to know quite what conditions they are prone to, but this knowledge could be a boon for our horticulture far beyond the specimens themselves, and I am pleased to note that the terms of our agreement will allow me to exploit this knowledge myself for the burnishment of my own reputation, and perhaps our mutual profit.

If all goes well with the final point of our negotiation, we shall be floating on the westward winds within a week.

In good spirits and with all respect, I remain,

your servant,
Rbt. Meriweather

Oh, Jack, I am in such a lather I can barely sit still to write this.

I hope I have done the right thing. I truly do. Today the negotiations concluded successfully, but two things give me pause. The first is that I have made one promise to the local head abbott that I do not fully comprehend, and surely it must be an error in the translation? But I have pledged to return the flowers to him if they do not thrive in our native land, as they believe the Occident to be cold and inhospitable. Indeed, I he spoke of these specimens in terms of an experiment, of testing their viability, so on that score we were in agreement. I assured him that I have the knowledge and the skills to keep any living thing thriving, so there will be no need for a return journey.

The second thing is, Jack, I had to give them a man: the engineer's mate, who will help them with their ship construction. Oh, assuredly, they said he would be sent home as soon as their own ship was built, such that they could undertake the journey, but how am I to know what his fate will be? However, heed this well: the forbidden flowers must be something truly special, something beyond my wildest imagining. For the man chosen did not want to stay in such an alien land *at first,* but to convince him they allowed him to enter the deepest inner secret garden. And after spending a few hours there, he chose gladly to remain!

He has just left the ship with all his worldly belongings in a chest, quite cheerful at his prospects! I admit his sudden change of heart worried me deeply as an icicle of fear pierced my optimism at last: what else but opium, or perhaps some narcotic elixir even stronger and more gripping to the weak man's soul could create such a change in him? I thought I had solved the mystery at last. But no, no, though he had been sworn to silence about what he had witnessed, he assured me that addictive substances have nothing whatever to do with it.

So. Tomorrow we shall receive the delivery, at last, of the blossoms themselves. They will be brought to us in the evening, such that we may again slip our moorings under the dark of night. I have supplied several monks with Wardian cases to collect the necessary herbs as well as the flowers themselves. God bless Nathaniel Ward and his ingenious invention! So long as the glass cases remain sealed, the tender plants inside need never be watered nor cared for on the journey, protected from cold, sea spray, invasion of fungus, and all other hazards to herbaceous life.

My heart races and my blood surges when I think on it. Tomorrow, at sunset, I will at last lay eyes on these blossoms that have inspired such devotion in the local populace and such covetous desire among our richest men.

To the Honorable, Esteemed, Heavenly, et cetera et cetera Abbott of the Tsang Mountain Lamasery—

My greatest gratitude to you and all the peoples of your realm for bestowing upon us the gift of your greatest treasure of which we shall endeavor to be worthy to receive at sunset today.

Oh God, Jack, I do not know what to think. I do not know what to do.

I will attempt to convey for you the gravity of the situation without resorting to crudeness, but you must forgive me if it cannot be done. Also, I have resorted to the whiskey you gave me before my sailing, which has remained untouched until now.

God help me.

At sunset, the Horizon had all banners flying, ready to unmoor, and a spacious and dry place in the hold prepared for the delivery. Quite a parade came down to the edge of the tea field from the lamasery, with the people chanting and singing and banging gongs—the sort of display we have seen before. All were dressed in silks so fine that the price of one of their tunics alone would feed a Westham family for a year, and up to the gangway pranced five princesses—for I know no other word that can possibly describe these women in their finery. Each wore an ensemble as brightly colored as an azalea, as multilayered as a peony, with her own hair crowning her head in improbable tiers, dappled with baubles, and each one led a contingent of three or four men bearing the Wardian cases and various chests, and once in the hold each one of these women directed the men where to put the cases. The Horizon crew watched all this with great interest, since if the weight of the cargo should grow too great we could be forced to other means of travel. However, these which they had brought did not seem to be too much for Horizon to handle, and soon Wu was thanking the women and ushering the men out.

Meanwhile, I confess my heart sank, for upon peering into the cases I saw nothing of exceptional beauty at all. Green herbs, some shot through with red, some small flowers here and there, nothing that bespoke of the mythic beauty of a "blossom of summer" and certainly nothing that looked like it warranted being forbidden to trade.

Again I thought perhaps these plants were something more powerful than the opium poppy, and that the illicit trade in addictive substances might be the purpose for the secrecy of my mission? But then why only five specimens? Why not try to seed an entire plantation, as they did when Mr. Fortune sought tea plants for the East India Company? I believe that expedition retrieved ten thousand seedlings, did they not?

I ordered the crew out, such that only I, the women, and the translator remained in the hold. *Show me the flowers that I came here for,* I insisted, and the translator struggled for a moment over the words. The women looked at one another with shy giggles.

Show me, I insisted again. Show me the blossom so beautiful that our navigator chose to stay behind in Tsang Rira. This time one of the women stepped forward and bowed to me, then stepped back.

Enraged now, I shook Wu by his shoulders and insisted he make it clear to them I wanted them to show me, that I might see with my own eyes, and yes, if I had to, touch with my own hands, these forbidden flowers, and that we would not leave until I was convinced of their beauty.

Wu translated haltingly, and then hid his face in his voluminous sleeves. I soon determined why. Each one of these princesses, their skin as smooth as cream and their clothes fit for royalty, gripped the hem of her tunic then and looked shyly up at me. I had no Earthly idea what they could mean by that.

And then, in unison, they lifted their dresses. They wore nothing underneath! One went so far as to use her fingers to expose a richness as ripe as a pomegranate to me, and at that I finally realized what I have done.

These women are the blossoms of summer.

The Most Honorable and Esteemed Terence Featherstone
Continental Occident Company
Wickham House
Grace Park

Dear Sir,

I write to you today in hopes that you will consider most keenly the exigencies of airship travel and the reasons to which I have turned what was planned to be a return voyage by sea into an overland airship journey of significant expense.

In the interest of the priorities put forth to my person by you, Sir, I deem it wise that our cargo not be handled by any more men than necessary. Indeed, I am quite certain that had we allowed our cargo to fall into the rough hands of a sea-going crew that the specimens would have been entirely spoilt regardless of what precautions I could take. It trust I need not overstate why the security of the Horizon is greatly preferable to that of a sea-going ship.

I am, as instructed, caring for the specimens personally, to ensure their delivery into your hands. I trust that the captain and crew of Horizon will be amply compensated for all they have done to ensure the success of the expedition.

With all respect, I remain,

your servant,
Rbt. Meriweather

Jack, we have just weathered a storm the likes of which can only be conceived in the turgid heat of these southern climes. Like a sailing ship, we are somewhat subject to the winds, and I feared as we neared the blackest cloud I have ever seen that lightning would be our undoing. But as Fate would have it, the Horizon was not struck, nor torn apart by hailstones, nor dashed into the sea by the gale.

In the light of morning, Jack, and in the clarity that comes after one's life has been endangered, I find myself reexamining both my orders and the conversations with officers of the Company I undertook prior to my sailing. In the end I must conclude that this is one monumental translation mistake.

If the directors of the Company had known, truly, that we would be trading in flesh, and if that were the reason for their vagueness and secrecy, why indeed would they have bothered to send an actual Botanist such as myself? Perhaps I may comprehend now, at least, the urgings of the abbott to whom I pledged I would return the Flowers to their land if they should wither or wilt?

How fortunate that I have been able to convince the crew, however, that these women are specially trained gardeners themselves and that our true cargo is in the herbs they bring along with them. The crew's main concern has been feeding and berthing so many people, but a section of the hold has been converted by the addition of hammocks and a curtained doorway into something resembling a cabin for the women. They are quite pleased with this arrangement and have taken to decorating the space with various of their colorful silks, and the shipwright has even created a hatch in the hull which they may open to peer out and to allow fresh air to circulate.

Meanwhile, we have spent the majority of the currency originally intended for the negotiation itself on resupply for the return voyage, as we will be passing over some inhospitable landscapes.

Make no mistake, though, these women are no gardeners. Indeed, one would say that their interests are not vegetal in the slightest, but carnal.

I discovered this that first night, when I woke to an unfamiliar sound, and thought for a moment that a stray animal must have crept aboard. The sound was repetitive, a kind of keening, and I slipped from my berth toward their quarters to investigate.

There I found such a sight, one of the women curled on the floor, and I revised my thought: surely she must be airsick, it being her first time aboard a craft such as Horizon. I knelt beside her to give her comfort, but she clutched at my hand, her lips as ripe and plump as a plum as she licked them, and then she licked at my finger before guiding it to the place where she blossomed.

With her tiny hands around my wrist, she encouraged me to manipulate her in such a way that her cries became less pained and more of a pant of effort. It soon became apparent to me that she reached a peak, much as a man would! I had no earthly idea that women could experience such ecstasy. Did you know this, Jack?

Could the altitude have an aphrodisiac effect, I wonder? Perhaps I shall try to broach the subject delicately with the captain, for when I returned to my cabin, my own flesh was in such a turgid state that I felt it urgently necessary to relieve myself in a similar manner.

Dear Diary,

Wu has brought me a gift from the "blossoms" that he indicated I should rub into my cheeks, some form of beautification salve. When, after a few days, I had not done so, the women took it upon themselves while we were taking the air upon the observation deck to cluster around me and coo and cluck with worry. They are continually fascinated by the fine hairs that rise upon my forearms whenever they stroke my skin lightly and equally concerned with my face. It has only just dawned on me as I sit to write this that perhaps they have never seen freckles before? It makes sense now: they are mistaking my natural sun speckles for a pox!

This is but a trifle, though, compared to the subject I must now record. I have found, truly, a subject that our scientific investigations have never before uncovered. Yet it is my curse that the knowledge should be something I can surely never publish? In the interest of science, however, I shall record my findings here nonetheless, in case the facts may some day be relevant in a world free of the social strictures imposed upon our society like a corset upon a body.

Recall that I was charged with the personal care of the specimens in my cargo by both my own Company orders and the promises made to their spiritual leader. How then, was I to react when one of the five women appeared to sicken during the voyage? She grew pallid and weak, and seemed unable to eat. I pressed Wu to interrogate them as to which of the herbs we were transporting with her might help her condition: they universally answered *none*.

This led to a fascinating side investigation into the herbs themselves. I have recorded their native names and drawings on the following page, along with the claims of the women, as to which one prevented pregnancy, which one prevented consumption. Another would prevent her from contracting syphilis! (Or so I believe the disease described by the women and Wu to be, under its rightful name.)

I have followed the publishing of Doctor William Grosvenor at St. Bartholomew's hospital avidly in recent years. The good doctor writes eloquently about how the average prostitute, rather than being ridden with disease as some might presume, is typically possessed of robust health—even more robust than wives and society ladies of good standing. He attributes this to a form of increased constitution gained through sensuality.

I myself would not have found this claim credible, but given my experiences aboard the Horizon, I have to concede there is some possibility that Grosvenor is correct. I have also formulated an additional hypothesis. In light of the botanical evidence I have gathered, it may be that there may be herbal treatments that the women of the night do not—perhaps *dare* not—share with their more innocent sistren, and keep to themselves for their sorority?

However, certainly the women under my care seem to wilt whenever they are not regularly experiencing ecstatic paroxysms. And when this even more severe case presented itself, in the form of Lily (for that is the name I gave her) falling acutely ill, I tried all other remedies first. When my herbal tinctures produced no positive effect, though, the women took charge of her from me, carrying her into their curtained-off section of the hold with much scolding.

I confess my curiosity got the better of me and I watched through a knothole in the deck above them to see what they would do.

I was amazed to watch as one of the women cradled her, while another lifted Lily's dress and manipulated her as I had done Rose on that first night they were in my charge. (Wu tried to teach me their names, but my tongue will not quite stretch around their native vowels and the women seem quite pleased with their new designations.) Soon she was tunneling into Lily's body with her fingers, though, jabbing her with a violence I would not previously have been certain a woman could withstand! Well, certainly not the frail, corseted creatures we are accustomed to, but these princesses, these blossoms, for all their delicate beauty, have a toughness and strength I can only compare to silk itself.

This treatment was apparently not sufficient, for soon, egged on by needy cries from Lily, Rose soon placed her hands at her own groin, making a sort of phallus of her fingers, and proceeded to emulate the motions and effect of a male partner.

I need not record, perhaps, that this sight astounded me, and indeed I hesitate to mention anything that could be construed as unsubstantiated by science. However, I postulate there must be some pheromonal component to such an action. Certainly it would not be unexpected for a male such as myself to achieve an erect state by such a visual presentation, and although I attempted to reduce my turgidity by means of repeating mathematical formulae in my mind, nothing could dissuade my blood from surging. I also experienced other effects that mere ocular input alone cannot elucidate, including elevated cardiac and respiratory activity, and one other telltale symptom—

That is to say I was not previously aware that it was possible that such an exposure alone could cause a man to spend, untouched, in his breeches.

This warrants further investigation.

Dear Jack,

I have discovered the true cause of the Opium War. Have you heard certain inadequacies to be inherent in Mandarin men? In the East, they believe the same of Occidentals! Meanwhile, the sword (or rifle) as proxy phallus seems universal. I trust I need say no more.

Yrs,
Rbt.

Dear Diary,

Lily recovered from her bout of illness, but Camellia followed suit. I was much disturbed to find the women berating my translator, and ultimately it became clear to me that they intended to banish him from their quarters. Understand I have learned a bit of their language, but not enough for diplomatic work, and meanwhile they have learnt only the most oft-used of our words, so I did not see how we could possibly have a medical discussion without him?

But they are quite clever with gestural communication, these women. I understand that from one valley to the next in the East the language may be entirely unintelligible, so perhaps they have more practice at it.

It was certainly clear enough they wanted me to undress. Ultimately I refused to disrobe, but I did agree to open my trousers for them. They clustered around me like curious cats around a bowl of cream. Before I could protest, they began investigating me with their hands as well as their eyes.

I frankly did not expect Rose's cry of startlement, nor the wide-eyed looks of the others. At first I thought it the ruddy color of my hair they found surprising. However, their gestures made it clear to me they considered my virility to be impressively sized. I had not previously known nor suspected myself of being particularly well-endowed. They conducted their investigations, as they did with the manipulations that I had witnessed, with wonder and not a whit of shame; It is clear to me that their customs and moires are entirely different from our own, so I took no offense at the handling of my person.

However, I did have a moment of apprehension when the others held my arms and urged Camellia forward. Her face reflected an unhealthy pallor, but as she took in the sight of my bared manhood, a sparkle seemed to appear in her eye. Her slim hand slipped around my girth and manipulated me to full erection, and her tongue darted between her lips as she observed a droplet of pre-ejaculate welling up.

I never dared to imagine that tender tongue would meet that swollen drop, but when she dipped her head downward, that is exactly what transpired before I could think to protest.

And upon observing the envigorating effect it had upon her—! Well, it would have been at best rude and at worst monstrous of me to deny her the apparent curative for her condition. Thus it was that I allowed her to suckle upon me like a kitten to a mama-cat's teat, never spending—heaven forfend!—for two days thereafter. It grew necessary for me at times to hold myself back through sheer will, dousing my own ardor with distasteful thoughts, as the nectar she craved was sweetest and most abundant immediately after my manhood would go from flaccid to fully straining.

However I must note for science that the effect of this treatment was ultimately only temporary. By the third day she was again wan and wasting. The ministrations of the others similarly had no beneficial effect.

She was clearly suffering and I could not bear to see her in need. I tried to ask the others what I could do, and their gestures made it clear to me they believed only one treatment could revive her sufficiently, one which I, being an as-yet unmarried man, should have been morally unencumbered to undertake.

Yet, I hesitated. To be absolutely certain of their intent, I spoke with Wu and upon learning that my interpretation was correct, I entreated him to undertake the deed. However he informed me quite regretfully that according to the rules and customs of their people, Camellia would only accept a man of her choosing—and she had previously rejected Wu quite vociferously. I found this idea preposterous at first as—to my mind—the libertine nature of the "blossoms" meant that they would be open to every form of sensual exploration irregardless of whom they might be with, but I was entirely mistaken in this conception.

But why me, I asked him, to which he replied that not only did the women trust me to be their caretaker, to see to their every need, but, he said: *you have shown yourself worthy in her eyes.* And, I admit, the knowledge of this brought a strange sort of warmth into my chest.

What else could I do? I took the dear girl to my cabin. Though she seemed content for me to perform the necessary duty upon the swept wood floor of the hold—attempting to part her thighs for me on the spot!—I myself lacked confidence that I could succeed under such conditions, with the other four women watching.

Once in my cabin, I seated her crossways in my sleeping hammock. It took only a few moments of manipulation for her flower to bloom, a redolent scent to rise, and her sap to glisten.

Do not ask where such an idea came into my head, but I wondered if perhaps the stimulation caused by friction and the cardiovascular effort spurred by it might be the true cause of the invigorating effect experienced by my charges, but as they seemed to believe mere digital manipulation to be inadequate, I did my best. Not even two tugs were necessary to bring me to attention givén the wanton display of her, and I allowed her to close her legs around my length as she swung back and forth on the hammock. Perhaps that alone would be enough, I dared hope, but as her cries grew more insistent and her movements more desperate, it was eventually impressed upon me that nothing short of fully penetrating her would do. Still, I held off as long as I could, until she seized me around the waist with her ankles and drove herself onto me, to be denied no longer.

She screamed when she reached her climax and—to my utter surprise—I did at that moment as well! (Climax, that is, not scream.) So focused was I on her that I suppose I was less than fully aware of my own state of arousal, but nonetheless, I have been given to understand that simultaneous paroxysms are rare in most couplings.

Perhaps I should attempt to train them to be silent should future medical treatments of this kind be necessary.

Dearest, dearest Livia,

I sit in reflection tonight to write you merely to assuage the longing in my heart, as we have been parted for over a year, but I am rapidly approaching home, as fleet as Mercury, bearing the promise that I shall always love you and care for you, no matter what exotic and bizarre rituals I might have witnessed, or participated in, upon such foreign and alien lands. You must promise never to ask of the ungodly things I encountered in my travels, and know that I love you with a pure heart. Memories of you sustain me through the most trying of circumstances.

Yours,
Robert

Dear Diary,

If I had fooled myself into thinking that my treatment of Camellia was to be unique, I was sorely mistaken. Within the space of a week, two of the others had cajoled me into also invigorating them in the same manner, although I suspect that Lily feigned her symptoms. I could not take the chance, though, that she might worsen, nor the rebellion that might ensue if I did not keep them satisfied.

Rose, though, sickened after a while, but refused to take me, even when the others insisted she should. I soon gathered that the objection was over the fact that I was, in her estimation, oversized. At a loss for what else to suggest, I once again suggested Wu? But no, they were all entirely opposed to Wu. I had the man over to my cabin to share a bit of port wine the captain had give me after the evening mess, and with his tongue warmed by alcohol he eventually elucidated for me that these five women had competed for the chance to come on this voyage. But whatever does that have to do with why they are uninterested in carnal relations with you, I asked. The answer was simply that after having sampled all the common fruits of their valley's own vines, they were tempted by the novelty to be found in the curve of a "banana" such as mine, or those of my countrymen.

In that case, I wondered if there might be one of the airmen she would try, if my manhood were too prodigious for her to accept? What ensued was the beginnings of my most scientific study to date, comparing height and weight of our subjects to the size of a man's virile organ.

The airmen were, fortunately, quite good natured about being measured in the name of research, being of the adventurous sort and also holding me in high esteem as a medical and scientific man. I measured them two at a time, ensuring that there should be no claims of impropriety on my part while alone with a man's equipment in hand, but they were all quite jolly on the whole. Interestingly enough, I was not the largest on board, but there were a few quite a bit smaller. (Wu himself also allowed himself to be measured. I must conclude that his size is not what the women objected to, as he was well within the average range, but that as he claimed, their objections were more along the lines of he was not as enticingly interesting as a specimen such as I.)

I brought the results of my survey to the women, who have learnt our numbers by now, and also effectively instructed them in the mathematics of standard deviation. They are wholly intelligent in both their abilities to grasp arithmetic concepts as well as to see reason, and their language acquisition is now proceeding speedily.

In the end Rose rejected the idea of taking one of the smaller airmen, but at least she overcame her fears upon realizing that I am not, in fact, freakishly outsized but merely in the top quintile of the likely range for human males.

Delivering Rose's treatment, however, was less straightforward than Camellia. Once Rose had accepted that no harm would come to her from my carnal phallic instrument, I thought I would bring her to my cabin and despatch my duty forthwith. However, that was not to be the case.

There was one I took to be slightly older than the others, whom I had dubbed Cloris, who then shooed the others out, leaving just me, her, and Rose in their curtained-off chamber. Cloris retrieved a jar of something from one of their chests and soon was coating my member with a most envigorating oil of some sort, pleasurable both in scent and sensation. I thought, at first, that she meant to convince Rose that the grease would ease the way, but then she bade me lie upon the floor and then climbed atop me!

Rose and she argued then, and in short order I found myself enveloped in an iron grip of hot velvet the likes of which I had not previously experienced. At first I attributed the sensation to my supine position, but I began to suspect other differences.

I lifted the edge of Cloris's garment, and though my mind froze with shock, my treacherous organ seemed only to grow stiffer with the realization that it was her fundament into which it plunged as she rose up and down upon it.

Nothing could have prepared me, either, for the fact that Cloris could reach climax exclusively from riding upon my member, her inner spasms nearly triggering mine as well. Nearly. She fell limp atop me for a few moments, and my hips pushed upward reflexively, seeking my own completion, but then she leapt free, and then subjected my genitalia to vigorous ablutions utilizing more concoctions from her jars. Once she was satisfied I was cleaner than a holystoned and well-swabbed quarterdeck, she returned to the grease once again.

Rose crawled closer then, and they sat on either side of me, each a hand on my chest, debating in quick, birdlike voices. I gather the thrust of the conversation was that if Cloris could do as she had, and gain such pleasure from it, then Rose could as well, if she feared for the integrity of her more traditional blossom.

The girl eventually straddled me, though I knew not then which of her entrances would be mine. Cloris made soothing noises at her, and then I felt the hot, wet silk of her settling against the tip of me.

She made even Cloris feel loose in comparison. The tension in her never relaxed, not the entire time she was working her way down over my shaft, which took considerable time as every half inch or so she would stop, her legs quivering. Once she was fully seated, she began to rock back and forth. I was mesmerized by the dance of pain and ecstasy across her face.

Cloris reached between Rose's legs to dandle her and I was grateful, for it was all I could do to press my palms against the airship's floor, holding still, as I would have considered it rude to thrust unexpectedly into her when she was still skittish.

When she came it was biting the back of her own hand, keeping silent as I'd taught, and her interior muscles pumping me as strongly as my own fist. I could not hold back my own flow then, and only kept myself from shouting by holding my breath, and the deprivation of oxygen may have caused me to lose consciousness for a moment.

She was relaxed, at last, when I came to, slumped atop me, but her skin was flushed and warm and her breathing even. Cloris and I put her back into her dress and then into her berth.

Rose's vigor is now entirely restored, but I fear for my own. These scientific inquiries can be taxing.

Jack, you are my dearest friend, and it is for that reason I feel compelled to inform you that even in the most detailed studies of human biology by the greatest naturalists of our nation I have never before seen described the capacity for pleasure that the female of our species holds. And make no mistake, although I could attempt to force myself to rationalize that these women are of an entirely different stock from our own, and trained in arts no good woman of standing would imagine, in the end the scientist in me is forced to two conclusions. One, women of all nations are entirely likely to share the features of these specimens, and two, our society is soulless in our denial of such ecstatic spiritual capacity! Perhaps you already knew this and—I am shamed to admit it—I have merely been hopelessly naïve?

Seeing the word upon the page now I realize but of course I have been naïve, in that I did not expect such an end to this mission, but... You know, Jack, that I have never visited a whore? When I was mastering my studies I had not the funds to spare, and then upon my travels in better men's circles I dared not assay anything which might damage my standing.

At any rate, I have learnt the most extraordinary ways to bring a woman to a healthful paroxysm. You may be laughing now as I describe what was entirely novel to me; perhaps you are already well versed in these techniques! I somehow suspect, though, that even you could benefit from this knowledge, as will any woman who enters your subsequent life. To that end, I shall attempt to describe the techniques that each woman loved best.

Rose, dear Rose, prefers my tongue tip to any other part of my body. A generous laving would reveal to me a tiny pearl, upon which I would suckle, and generous milk would flow forth from her loins when I did. One must not suckle too hard, for that produces pain that can only be soothed by long, gentle strokes of the tongue, which action can become quite fatiguing to a man's jaw. (Note that with many physical exertions, of course, one can become accustomed to them with practice.)

Cloris, of course, could achieve climax by manipulation of her fundament, but I was astonished to learn that any of them could, though it was only the preferred method of Cloris and Camellia. Cloris, I found, could climax but once, while the others could repeat the endeavor again and again! Camellia, sweet Camellia, could climax multiple times by manipulation of her hidden pearl, as well as both forms of penetration. In fact, she is the one who is brought most quickly to climax by a combination of all three forms of stimulation achieved by my member in her fundament, a pair of digits into her womanly cavern, and my free hand massaging her exterior.

If one were to take only Rose and Camellia as examples, however, one might think that these women might never have need of a man, for manipulation by finger as well as fashioned phallus seems to serve most of their needs if plied skillfully. However, I was similarly astonished to find that Azalea and Peony cannot, in fact, reach climax without some form of insertion, and sweet Peony cannot achieve completion at all unless it is the manly staff itself which serves her!

With such variety and variation in just the forms of these five, how many more wonders of pleasure and vigor might yet be found among the women of our own blood?

I find myself as reassured of the necessity of marriage as we know it as I am of the necessity for regular stimulation of the female organs for purposes beyond procreation. Understand me well, Jack. No woman that you care for should ever need suffer the hysteria, nervousness, wasting, or listlessness that the fair sex are prone to, should you take it upon yourself to care for her properly! Oh Jack, you know I should never direct you in moralistic fashion, but do bear my discoveries in mind, for I have no doubt that your own happiness as well as that of your intended shall be assured by this exotic method if practiced discreetly!

Dear Diary,

I must sheepishly confess that over the past month or so of our journey, as I have grown to know the "blossoms" better and better, that my concern over their wellbeing once they are out of my care has been steadily increasing. For, after all, in what way is this transport of them not that most abhorrent of practices, the trading in flesh? Cloris in particularly has gained the most language and I finally spoke to her of my concern that the fate that awaits them is at best the life of a courtesan and at worst as whores. She took my concerns most lightly, however, and explained her belief that she and her sistren would be choosing husbands upon establishing themselves in London, facilitated secretly by the Company! At first I took this to be a delusion, but I grow more and more convinced that she is correct and it is my own naivete and assumptions that have kept me from realizing the truth.

I write this from the deck of the Queen of the Horizon as the coast of Sweden hoves into view. The dawn sky is golden, tinged with pink, and the towering clouds look nearly like the tall bluffs of red sandstone that line the Tsang Valley. We will be docking in Copenhagen for a few days for repairs but I shall not be joining the crew on their brief furlough; I shall stay behind with the "blossoms" and administer the necessary treatments to them, and to serve as their guard, though in truth knowing what I do now, I doubt that any marauder who might happen onto the ship with ill intent would leave again alive.

The reason for our repairs is the pirate attack we repelled over the Baltic Sea. Our watch first spotted a brigantine dirigible and took it for a friendly Hungarian air-navy representative, then lost it in the clouds. By the time we heard the rattle of her propellers it was too late to flee and a boarding party came at us on gliders. Fortunately for us, our long cannon took out their main lift cells and only a few of them made it on board before their retreat. One of these marauders, however, breached our hull not far from the Blossoms' makeshift cabin.

I needn't have worried, as by the time I hurried to their "rescue" they had quite handily despatched the intruder using no weapon other than their bare hands! This, more than anything, convinces me that my preconceived notions of what the feminine form is capable of have been shaped by a lack of data and—it must be admitted—*bias.* The same is true of my underestimation of the ambition and character of the Blossoms, and it now seems to me impossible that any man should be capable of impressing his will upon them without their agreement.

I am certain I will not be the last man to underestimate them, but my hopes for their prospects only rise along with my esteem. Indeed, I must at this point expect that they will be taking my home country by storm.

The Most Honorable and Esteemed Terence Featherstone
Continental Occident Company
Wickham House
Grace Park

Dear Sir,

I am pleased to report to you the unalloyed success of my mission to retrieve the "summer blossoms" of Tsang Valley. All five specimens have survived their transport with their beauty and health fully retained owing to the vigorous efforts on my part to maintain them thus.

A note to their new caretakers. These flowers require special handling to retain their vigor. Just as a healthy hedge must be pruned regularly, these too require some care that might seem unorthodox at first. I trust that their caretakers will find this task pleasurable rather than onerous.

Their petals require spreading or they will not come to full blossom. I recommend this at least once a day to ensure their sap runs clear.

At least once a week they also must be fertilized.

Your servant,
Robert Meriweather

Livia, dearest Livia,

I send this ahead by air courier that you might meet me at our new home in Somerset. We have but to cross the North Sea and then I shall once again stand upon our native soil! We are re-provisioning the airship here and will follow in a few days. The representatives of the Continental Occident Company will be expecting your arrival. I shall write to your father as well, but I wanted to include this letter to you, my love, with news of my success.

I shall make you the happiest woman in the world.

Yours eternally,

Robert

Author's Note

The idea for this book was inspired partly from the real historical account of adventuring botanist Robert Fortune—yes, that was his real name—who was sent to China to steal the secrets of tea cultivation. Sarah Rose has written a nonfiction book about him entitled *For All The Tea in China,* if you want to know more about Fortune in particular, but apparently the adventuring naturalist was something of a thing, back in the day.

Also taken from the historical record are the bits about Dr. Grosvenor's writings about prostitutes in Victorian England and his bafflement that his studies showed that the ladies of the night suffered fewer venereal diseases than other women, rather than more. I think I have the Whores of Yore account on Twitter to thank for that one!

This book was, of course, NOT written to celebrate or excuse the fact that the Asian female body has been fetishized, colonized, commodified, and controlled by western imperial powers for centuries. As an erotica writer, I often explore power dynamics and the ways in which sexual agency often moves counter to expectations. As an Asian woman myself, I wanted to turn some of the tropes inside out, where the white man essentially becomes the sexual servant of the women rather than the other way around. One of my favorite things about steampunk is that the genre creates a space to refashion and reboot history. While this is just an erotic novella, I've tried to telegraph how in my steamy-punk version of the world, things are not going to turn out for the British Empire the way they did in real life. I hope you enjoyed these musings.

About the Author

Cecilia Tan is an award-winning author of passionate fiction. *RT Book Reviews* awarded her Career Achievement in Erotic Romance in 2015 and her novel *Slow Surrender* (Hachette/Forever, 2013) won the RT Reviewers Choice and the Maggie Award. She is the author of the Secrets of a Rock Star series (Hachette/Forever), the Magic University series (Riverdale Avenue Books), and *Daron's Guitar Chronicles* (self-published), among many other works. Cecilia also founded the Fetish Fair Fleamarket in the early 1990s and after directing the event for over two decades, is now retired from BDSM event-running. You can still find her getting her kink on at the occasional BDSM, anime, or science fiction convention, though.

Visit CeciliaTan.com to learn more, or to join her Patreon or to subscribe to her email newsletter.